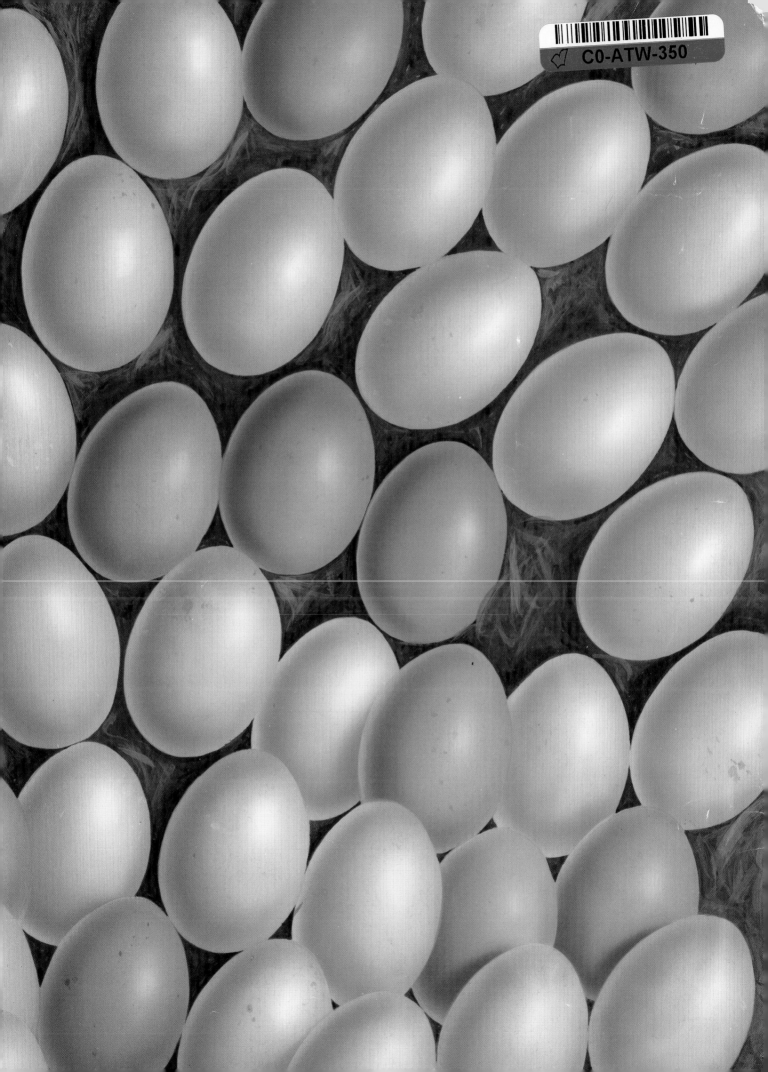

First published in Switzerland under the title *Teddy bei den Osterhasen*.

No part of this publication may be reproduced in whole or in part,
or stored in a retrieval system, or transmitted in any form or by any means,
electronic, mechanical, photocopying, recording, or otherwise, without written
permission of the publisher. For information regarding permission, write to
North-South Books, Inc., 1123 Broadway, Suite 800, New York, NY 10010.

ISBN 0-439-41115-7

12 11 10 9 8 7 6 5 4 3 2 1   2 3 4 5 6 7/0

Printed in the U.S.A.   24

First Scholastic printing, March 2002

Teddy's
Easter Secret

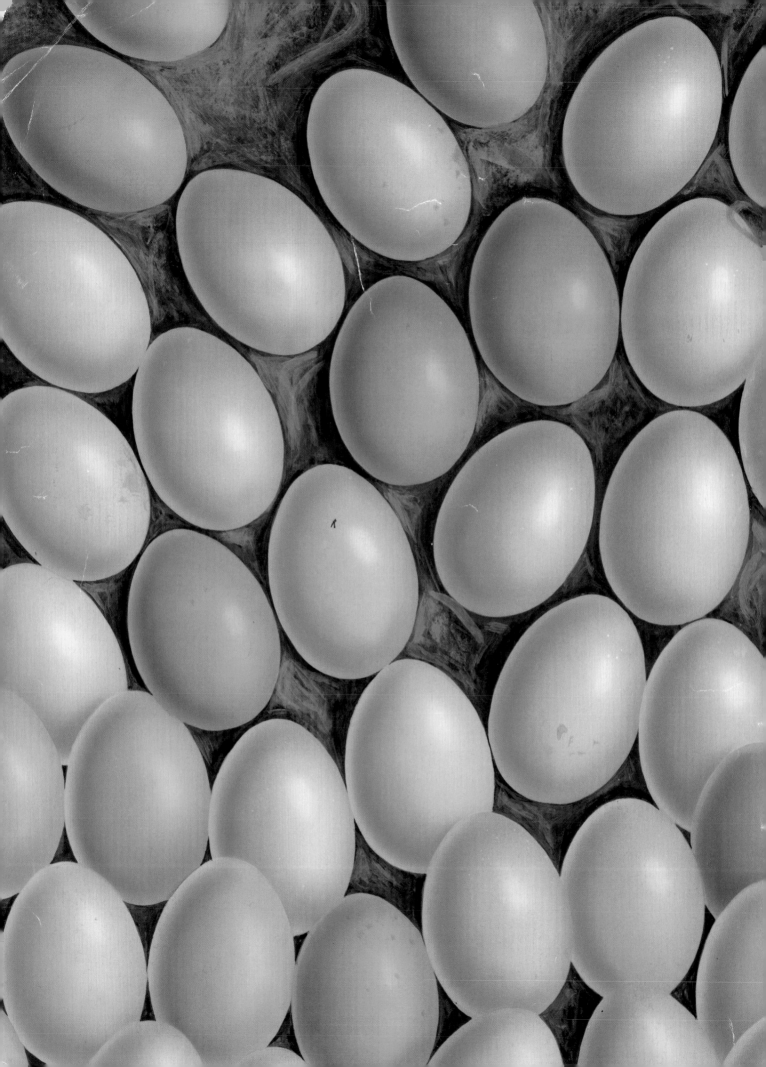

Teddy's Easter Secret

By Gerlinde Wiencirz

Illustrated by Giuliano Lunelli

Translated by J. Alison James

SCHOLASTIC INC.

New York Toronto London Auckland Sydney
Mexico City New Delhi Hong Kong Buenos Aires

Teddy was angry! Paul had left him behind in the sandbox.

They had been playing together so nicely. They'd built a
castle and dug a long tunnel. Then Paul got hungry and ran
into the house.

Gradually it grew dark. Teddy should have been snuggled up
in Paul's warm bed. But here he was in the cold sand, tired and
all alone.

Suddenly he heard rustling noises.

The sound came from the henhouse. Carefully, Teddy peered over the rim of the sandbox. It might be a fox, he thought. But the hens were silent. The rooster didn't even crow. Their silence was more mysterious than the soft noises.

Then Teddy saw something amazing. A rabbit ran out of the henhouse carrying a basket filled with eggs. What could a rabbit do with all those eggs? Teddy wondered.

Without thinking, Teddy jumped up and ran after the rabbit. But by the time he was through the trees behind the house, the rabbit had almost disappeared over the hill.

Teddy stood for a moment, unsure about what to do. Then the moon slipped out from behind a cloud, and he could clearly make out the rabbit's tracks in the damp grass. He followed the footprints to the edge of the woods.

It was dark in the woods. Teddy did not like it one bit.

A voice hooted down, making him jump. "Who are you, and what are you doing?"

Teddy looked up and saw an owl. "I'm solving a mystery," said Teddy, and he told the owl what had happened.

"I see," said the owl. "Don't you know what day tomorrow is?"

"Yes, I do," said Teddy. "Tomorrow is Easter."

"That clue is as important as your rabbit tracks," said the owl. "Come with me."

She brought Teddy to the top of a hill where they could see beyond the woods. "Do you see that lone pine standing on the crest?" asked the owl. "If you follow the maple trees through the woods, then climb the hill to the pine, you'll be well on your way."

"But what then?" asked Teddy.

The owl just turned her head all the way around and whispered, "It's a secret."

The forest was horribly dark and scary. Every creaking branch and fluttering bat made Teddy freeze. A mouse dashed by his feet, and Teddy leapt into a tree.

Then he laughed at himself. How silly he was to be scared of a little mouse just because it was dark! Feeling braver, he went on. It wasn't so much further to that big pine tree.

A branch snapped, and two large eyes glowed in the darkness. It was a fox! Teddy held his breath and tried to blend into the tree bark.

Foxes ate hens and eggs and rabbits! Had that fox feasted on his rabbit? But the fox slunk right past, so Teddy went on.

Finally he was out of the woods, and there on the hill was the lone pine. Now what was he to do? He spied a narrow path that led through a row of wild raspberries, and bending low, Teddy slipped through.

Before him lay an enchanted meadow filled with busy rabbits painting thousands of eggs.

"Who are you, and what are you doing?"

Teddy looked up, surprised. A large old rabbit was glaring at him.

"I think I've solved the mystery," Teddy said, smiling happily. "You must be—"

"The Easter Bunny," said the old rabbit, still a bit gruff.

"I am Teddy. And I'm ever so pleased to meet you. You see, I saw a small rabbit run away with our eggs, so I followed him here."

"We'll have to be more careful," said the Easter Bunny. "But now what should we do with you?" He scratched himself thoughtfully behind the ear. "Since you've discovered our secret, you might as well help us get ready."

So on that magical night, Teddy got to work alongside the Easter Bunny's helpers, painting eggs for the children.

"Where do you get the paints?" asked Teddy.

"We mix them ourselves from tree bark and leaves, blossoms and plant juice," said the Easter Bunny. "Be sure that no two eggs are alike. We pride ourselves on making each one unique. And be careful of the dye, it doesn't wash out easily."

Teddy promised to be careful, but soon he forgot.

"Yikes! Watch out!" cried the little rabbit. Too late! Teddy had a thick blue splotch on his cheek.

They filled up baskets with the painted eggs, and then the Easter Bunny passed out the addresses of the children.

He gave Paul's basket to the little rabbit. "And take Teddy with you," he said, "so he doesn't get lost in the woods."

Then the Easter Bunny took Teddy aside. "Now you must promise me that you will never share our secret with anyone."

"Not even the hens?" asked Teddy. "Not even Paul?"

The Easter Bunny shook his head. "Not anybody."

Teddy thought of all the wonderful things he'd seen and done that night, and how he could remember them even without talking. He nodded. "All right," he promised. "I won't tell."

Then Teddy and the little rabbit set off.

"What if we see the fox?" asked Teddy.

"Foxes leave us alone at Easter," the little rabbit said with a laugh.

The basket was rather heavy, so Teddy and the rabbit took turns carrying it.

"Now you can be an Easter Teddy," joked the little rabbit.

The sun was already coming up when they climbed over the fence.

"We have to hide the eggs well," said Teddy. "Paul is good at finding them." When they were finished, the little rabbit waved good-bye and disappeared among the trees.

Only then did Teddy notice how tired he was. He had been out all night long. He curled up again in a corner of the sandbox and fell fast asleep.

He slept until the sun had risen high into the sky. He was still sleeping when Paul took him in his arms. And he pretended to be asleep when Paul asked, "Teddy, how did you get that blue spot on your cheek?"

Teddy wanted to tell Paul all about his adventures, but he had promised to keep the Easter Bunny's secret. So he kept his eyes closed and snuggled deep into Paul's arms, while Paul searched high and low to find his beautiful Easter eggs.